THIS WALKER BOOK BELONGS TO:

_____

_____

_____

_____

For Stephen and Kevin and Elias
With appreciation for the
work of Hope Ryden
≰ **J.L.**

For Andrew
≰ **B.F.**

First published 1998 by Walker Books Ltd
87 Vauxhall Walk, London SE11 5HJ

This edition published 1999

2 4 6 8 10 9 7 5 3 1

Text © 1998 Jonathan London
Illustrations © 1998 Barbara Firth

This book has been typeset in Veronan.

Printed in Hong Kong

British Library Cataloguing in Publication Data
A catalogue record for this book is
available from the British Library.

ISBN 0-7445-6966-4

AT THE
EDGE
OF THE
FOREST

Jonathan London

illustrated by
Barbara Firth

WALKER BOOKS
AND SUBSIDIARIES
LONDON · BOSTON · SYDNEY

Winter came on a burst
of wind, and the snow
turned the world white.

That was the year the sheep
had to be scooped from snow
and bundled into the barn
to keep from freezing.

That was the year of the coyotes.

One blue day after a storm,
I woke to hear the sheep
baaing in the barn.
   On my way there, I saw tracks.
      Deep holes along the fence line.
      There were chores to be done
         but curiosity had caught me.

I snowshoed towards the edge of the forest,
  leaving our small farm behind.
I stopped to catch my breath.

And there ahead I saw it – and then I didn't.
Something fast and bushy and golden brown –
  then gone.
Coyote. I knew it.

Dad had said there were coyotes about.

"If they come too close they'll be dead.
  Coyotes kill sheep," he said.

I trudged on, searching
    for tracks in the deep snow.
The wind bit my face
    as I came upon a meadow.
And there below was Coyote.
He froze and I froze, too.
He lifted one paw
    and cocked his head,
    listening.

Suddenly he pounced
    on his own shadow and dived
    head first into the snow.
Only the black tip of his tail stuck out.
Then he popped up –
    as if grinning – with a mouse!

When he saw me he froze again,
then took off like a streak
of furred lightning.
My eyes burned with that
glimpse of Coyote.
I was slow to turn back home.

Spring came
  and I saw no sign of him.
Then one day just before dawn
  the cries of the sheep awoke us.
We scrambled into clothes
  and out into the grey light.
Sheep scattered like
  huge balls of cotton.
  We found tufts of wool dyed
  blood red. Dad counted lambs
  and found one missing.
"Coyote," he said, and gazed out
  towards the dark forest.

When he got his shotgun
I thought about what he'd said
about coyotes coming too close.

We followed signs – drops
of blood, fur on a thistle,
prints in spring mud.
Dad was a great tracker.
But with his long strides
it was hard to keep up.
My heart raced, but my legs
raced even faster.

On Lindbergh's Hill we looked down,
    and there they were.
Coyote and another, nose to nose,
    some well-chewed meat
    on the ground between.
Dad raised his gun and took aim.

The coyotes licked muzzles
    and I blurted, "Look, Dad!
    The coyotes are kissing!"

Dad hesitated, but his finger
held the trigger and
began to squeeze.

I covered my ears.

Just then four pups
tumbled out of scrub willow
and swarmed their parents,
wagging and yipping for life.
"It's a family, Dad!" I shouted.
"Coyote brought them food!"

Dad didn't budge, but his eyes
were squeezed shut. Finally
he lowered his gun and looked at me.
"It's time we found a big shepherd dog
to run our fence," he said.
"We're a family, too."
And we headed for home.

That night,
  for the first time,
  we heard the coyotes sing.
And now, whenever we hear
  their eerie song,
  our dog howls back.
And sometimes
  I howl with him.

MORE WALKER PAPERBACKS
For You to Enjoy

LET THE LYNX COME IN
by Jonathan London/Patrick Benson

In the middle of a snowy wilderness, a small boy and a
giant lynx embark on a magical moonlit adventure…

0-7445-6041-1   £4.99

WHAT NEWT COULD DO FOR TURTLE
by Jonathan London/Louise Voce

Turtle is always helping Newt and saving him from danger. "That's what
friends are for!" he says. But Newt feels embarrassed: if only there
were something *he* could do for Turtle… Then one day there is.

"A big, inviting book about friendship and gratitude…
This is a lovely book… Highly recommended." *Naomi Lewis, The Evening Standard*

0-7445-5493-4   £4.99

WE LOVE THEM
by Martin Waddell/Barbara Firth

Two children love their pet rabbit and their dog Ben. But Ben is growing old…
"Introduces death naturally and matter-of-factly … will bear
repeated readings." *Susan Hill, The Sunday Times*

0-7445-7256-8   £4.99

Walker Paperbacks are available from most booksellers, or by post from B.B.C.S., P.O. Box 941, Hull, North Humberside HU1 3YQ

24 hour telephone credit card line 01482 224626

To order, send: Title, author, ISBN number and price for each book ordered, your full name and address, cheque or
postal order payable to BBCS for the total amount and allow the following for postage and packing:
UK and BFPO: £1.00 for the first book, and 50p for each additional book to a maximum of £3.50.
Overseas and Eire: £2.00 for the first book, £1.00 for the second and 50p for each additional book.

Prices and availability are subject to change without notice.